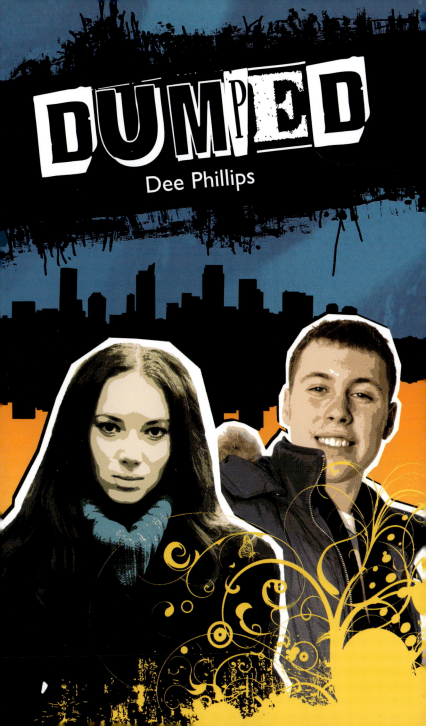

DUMPED

Dee Phillips

RiGHT NOW!

Blast
Dare
Dumped
Fight
Goal
Grind
Joyride
Scout

First published by Evans Brothers Limited

2A Portman Mansions, Chiltern Street, London W1U 6NR, United Kingdom

Copyright © Ruby Tuesday Books Limited 2009

This edition published under license from Evans Limited

All rights reserved

© 2011 by Saddleback Educational Publishing

ISBN-13: 978-1-61651-247-7
ISBN-10: 1-61651-247-4

Printed in Guangzhou, China
0112/CA21200022

16 15 14 13 12   2 3 4 5 6 7

I have to talk to Ryan.
I have to talk to him tonight.
But I don't know what to say to him.
Tonight, I have to make a choice.

DUMPED

ONE MOMENT CAN CHANGE YOUR LIFE FOREVER

It's very cold tonight.
My feet are cold.
My hands are cold.
I'm waiting in the park.
I'm waiting for Ryan.

4

Come on, Ryan. Where are you?

I jump up and down.
It's so cold.
Where are you, Ryan?

Why do you always have to be late?

Where r u Ryan?

I have to talk to Ryan.
I have to talk to him tonight.

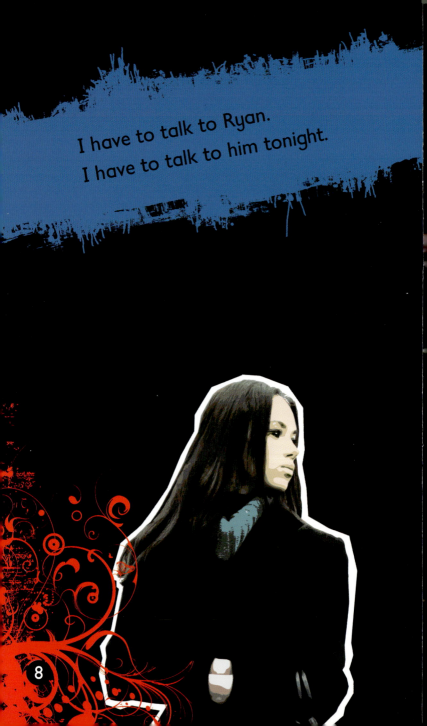

But I don't know what to say to him.
Tonight, I have to make a choice.

Ryan is my boyfriend.
We've been going out for three years.
I love Ryan.
But does he love me?

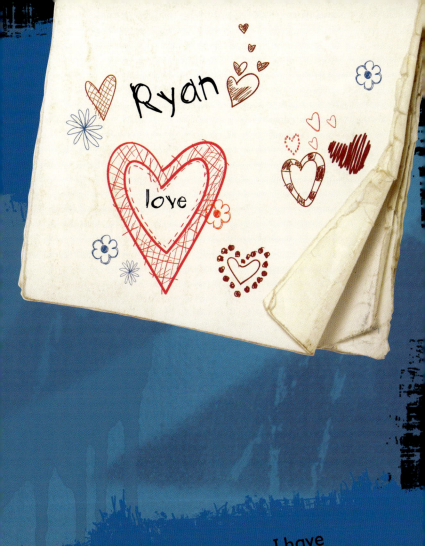

I need to know because I have
to make a choice.

This is my choice.
Stay in Philadelphia with Ryan.

Or start a new life in California

Dad's job is moving to California.

Dad thinks I should go with him to California.

He thinks I'm too young to stay in Philly on my own.

Brittany is my best friend.
Brittany thinks life will be better in California, too.
Brit says, "You are SO lucky, Kayla."
She made a list.

Philly

rain
white skin
college
work
Ryan

California

sun
suntan
beach
beach parties
buff surfers

Brittany says, "Go to California. Tell Ryan he is SO dumped."

I made another list.

So that's why I'm waiting.
Waiting for Ryan in the cold park.

Do you love me, Ryan?
I need to know.
Because sometimes it's hard to tell.

21

Dad says, "That boy is a waste of space!"

Brittany says, "Ryan acts like your brother, not your boyfriend."

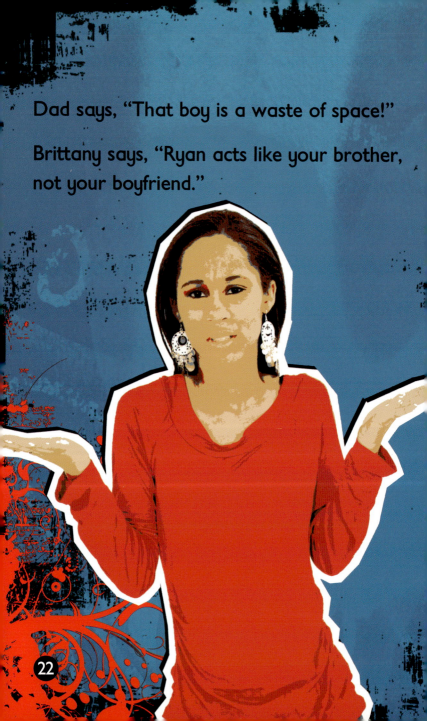

I say, "Do you love me, Ryan?"
Ryan just gives me his funny smile.

Ryan sent me a Valentine's card.
Once.

I jump up and down.
It's so cold.
Where are you, Ryan?

Ryan is always late.

Dad says, "That boy needs to get his act together."

Brit says, "That guy has NO respect for you."

All I do is wait—all the time. Last week I was waiting outside the movies. Tonight, I'm waiting for Ryan in the cold park.

29

A new life in California.

Dad says, "Forget about Ryan.
Life will be better in California."

Brittany says, "Forget about Ryan.
Think about all those buff surfers."

I jump up and down.
My feet are cold.
My hands are cold.
Ryan is thirty minutes late.

No new messages

Where are you, Ryan?

Dad is right. Brittany is right.
I've made my choice.
I'm going to California.

No more cold.
No more waiting.
Tonight, Ryan is dumped!

35

I feel good that I've made a choice.
But I feel sad, too.
I will miss Ryan a lot.

But will he miss me?

Here he comes.
He looks cold.
He looks happy.
I feel cold.
Cold and sad.

But life will be better in California.

I will find a new guy in California.

A new guy who loves me.

Ryan stands in front of me.
He looks down at me.
He holds out his hand.
There's a key in his hand.
Ryan says, "I'm sorry I'm late.
I had to pick this key up for you."

He says, "It's a key for Aunt Judy's House. Mom & Aunt Judy say you can stay there."

Ryan smiles his funny smile.

"Don't go," he says.

"Please stay."

DUMPED—WHAT'S NEXT?

WORK IT OUT
ON YOUR OWN

Kayla makes lists to help her make a choice.
What choice might you have to make? For example:

Ryan

good kisser   makes bad jokes
always happy   always late
funny smile   bad music taste
I love him   does he love me?

- Going to see a band you don't like but all your friends do.
- Sticking up for somebody who is being bullied.
- Buying something expensive but that you really want.

List the reasons for and against your choice.

COFFEE BREAK
WITH A PARTNER

Role-play two of the characters meeting for coffee the next day. Choose from Dad, Ryan, Brittany or Kayla. Think about the conversation they would have:

- What would they discuss?
- How would they feel?
- What advice would be given?
- How would that advice be taken?

What do you think Kayla should do? In your group, discuss what you would do in her situation. You could think about some of these questions:

- Is Kayla too young to stay in Philadelphia on her own?
- Is she too young to settle down?
- Should she finish college in Philadelphia? Or would she learn more by transferring to California?
- Does Ryan really love Kayla?

THE COLOR RED
ON YOUR OWN / WITH A PARTNER / IN A GROUP

Look at how the color red is used in the book's design. What does red make you think of? Love, anger, lips, blood, roses…

Make up sentences beginning with *"Red is…"*

- Organize your sentences to create a poem.
- Make a performance of your poem.

The color red

Red is the anger I feel when people put me down.

45

IF YOU ENJOYED THIS BOOK, TRY THESE OTHER RiGHT NOW! BOOKS.

Taylor hates this new town. She misses her friends. There's nowhere to skate!

Today is Carlos's tryout with Chivas. There's just one place up for grabs. But today, everything is going wrong!

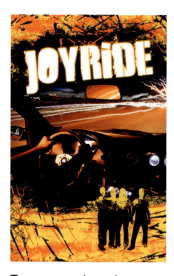

Tanner sees the red car. The keys are inside. Tanner says to Jacob, Bailey and Hannah, "Want to go for a drive?"

FIGHT

It's Saturday night.
Two angry guys. Two knives.
There's going to be a fight.

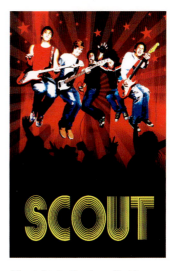

SCOUT

Tonight is the band's big
chance. Tonight, a record
company scout is at their gig!

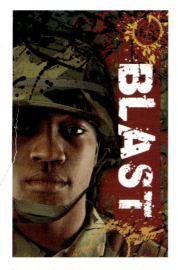

BLAST

Damien's platoon is under
attack. Another soldier is in
danger. Damien must risk
his own life to save him.

DARE

It's just an old, empty house.
Kristi must spend the night
inside. Just Kristi and the
ghost...